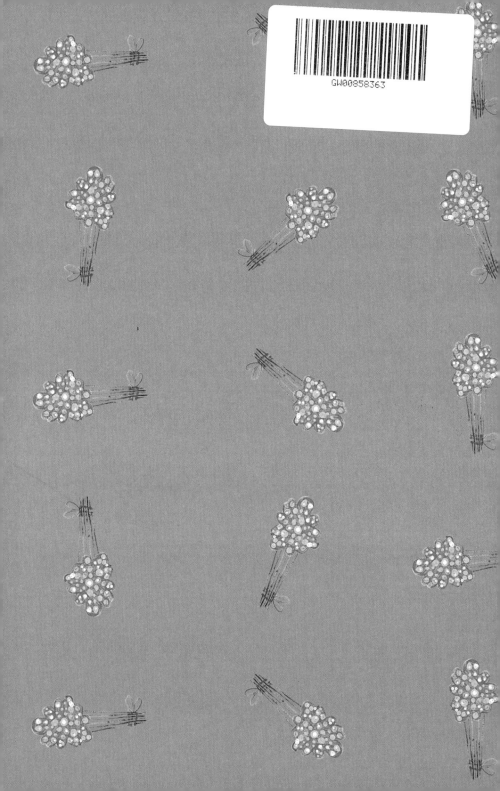

In Trouble with **Primrose Paws**

For Jasmine
R.I.

For Daisy
M.W.

Reading Consultant: Prue Goodwin, Lecturer in literacy and children's books

ORCHARD BOOKS
338 Euston Road, London NW1 3BH
Orchard Books Australia
Hachette Children's Books
Level 17/207 Kent Street, Sydney NSW 2000

First published in 2011 by Orchard Books

Text © Rose Impey 2011
Illustrations © Melanie Williamson 2011

ISBN 978 1 40830 221 7 (hardback)
ISBN 978 1 40830 229 3 (paperback)

1 3 5 7 9 10 8 6 4 2 (hardback)
1 3 5 7 9 10 8 6 4 2 (paperback)

Printed in China

Orchard Books is a division of Hachette Children's Books,
an Hachette UK company.

www.hachette.co.uk

Nipper McfeE

In Trouble with Primrose Paws

Written by ROSE IMPEY

Illustrated by MELANIE WILLIAMSON

ORCHARD BOOKS

Nipper McFee was in love.
And love meant trouble with
a capital 'T'.

When Nipper first saw Primrose
Paws, he thought she was the
cat's whiskers. His stomach
did somersaults. He didn't feel
a bit hungry.

But worst of all: Nipper lost
all interest in catapults.
His friends, Will and Lil, thought
he must be getting cat flu.

But Nipper wasn't ill – he was in love. For the first time in his life, Nipper felt shy. He felt far too shy to speak to Primrose Paws.

"If you can't tell her," said Will,
"give her a present."
"*Flowers*," advised Lil.

But Nipper was
broke, as usual.

Mrs McFee had stopped his pocket
money again.

So Nipper had to be on his best behaviour *all* week.

11

Finally Nipper had saved up
enough money. He went to
Mr Mewler's corner shop and
bought the best flowers – *catmint*.

Soon, Nipper's old enemies – the
basement rats – discovered his
secret. Now they had a new plan
to *Get Nipper*!

They wrote a love letter to
Primrose Paws and pretended
it was from Nipper.

It was a very scruffy letter –
full of mistakes and crossings out.

Primrose Paws didn't like the letter. When she read it, she blushed under her fur.

Then she screwed it up and threw it in the bin.

Nipper knew nothing about the letter.
When he gave Primrose Paws the
flowers, she threw those in the bin, too.

Nipper was very disappointed.

"Maybe she doesn't like flowers,"
Will suggested.

"Maybe she gets hay fever," said Lil.

Nipper hadn't thought of that.

Next time he would buy a different
present. Nipper started to save
up again.

But the rats had another trick up
their pesky sleeves.
They sent a second letter to
Primrose Paws asking her to meet
Nipper in the park after school.

Primrose Paws was even madder now. She *would* meet Nipper. This time, she would give *him* a present: a big piece of her mind!

But when she got to the park, there was no sign of Nipper – or anyone else. Suddenly, the rats rushed out and surrounded her.

"What do you want?" she demanded.
But the rats just stood around
squeaking with laughter.
Primrose Paws felt a little bit scared.

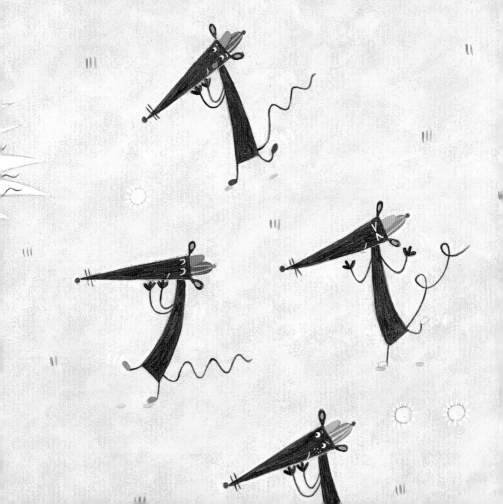

This time, Nipper had bought some
balloons. He was on his way home
with them when he saw the love of
his life surrounded by his enemies.

Nipper hid behind a tree to find out
what was going on.

The rats were planning to tie
Primrose Paws to a tree.
"That idiot Nipper will soon give
us all his pocket money just to get
you back," they squeaked.

Nipper almost rushed out to save her.
But then he thought of a better plan.

He curled his claws and burst
the balloons . . .
Bang! Bang! Bang! Bang!

The rats nearly jumped out of
their skins with fright. They ran
off squealing . . .

Now, Nipper could think of nothing but Primrose Paws. He even dreamed about her. Will and Lil were getting *bored*.

But then, one day, Nipper woke up!
He ate a *huge* breakfast, then
he went to look for his catapult.
At last he seemed to have forgotten
all about love.

"Thank goodness for that," said
Will, and Lil agreed.

ROSE IMPEY   MELANIE WILLIAMSON

All priced at £8.99

Orchard Books are available from all good bookshops,
or can be ordered from our website: www.orchardbooks.co.uk,
or telephone 01235 827702, or fax 01235 827703.

Prices and availability are subject to change.